The United Nations

ITS HISTORY AND THE CANADIANS WHO SHAPED IT

FIFTY YEARS OF STRUGGLE AND HOPE

Desmond Morton

KIDS CAN PRESS LTD.

TORONTO

To Patrick, Emily and all the children of Canada who have been born and grown up without experiencing the scourge of war.

Acknowledgements

Authors know better than anyone that books are a collective project. Liz MacLeod had the original idea and made the final editorial correction. In between, Susan Glover, Jamie Findlay and Evan Bergstra supplied ideas and Kathie Hill, Marie-Louise Moreau and Suzanne Aubin got on with the rest of my work so I had time to write a book. As for the book's limits and faults, they are the author's responsibility alone.

Kids Can Press Ltd. acknowledges with appreciation the assistance of the Canada Council and the Ontario Arts Council in the production of this book.

Kids Can Press Ltd. acknowledges the financial support of the Government of Canada through the Canadian Studies and Special Projects Directorate.

Canadian Cataloguing in Publication Data
Morton, Desmond, 1937–
    The United Nations : Its history and the Canadians who shaped it

Includes index
ISBN 1–55074–222–1

1. United Nations – Juvenile literature.   2. United Nations   Canada – Juvenile literature.   I. Title.

JX1977.Z8M67 1995   j341.23   C95–931203–X

Text copyright © 1995 by Desmond Morton

Kids Can Press Ltd.
29 Birch Avenue
Toronto, Ontario, Canada
M4V 1E2

Edited by Elizabeth MacLeod
Photos researched by Natalie Pavlenko Lomaga
Designed by Counterpunch/Linda Gustafson
Printed and bound in Canada

95 0 9 8 7 6 5 4 3 2 1

Photo credits
Canapress Photo Service: 28. **Department of National Defence**: 27 (top and bottom left), 30, 31. **First Light**: 32–33 (Eric Curry). **International Civil Aviation Organization**: 6. **Kell Isfeld**: 27 (right). **Yvonne Kupsch**: 17 (right). **National Archives of Canada**: 14–15 (background – PA3153), 16 (Donald I. Grant/PA 115578). **The Population Council**: 35 (right – Jill Krementz). **Quebec Urban Community Tourism and Convention Bureau**: 55 (right). **Jean Steckle**: 37. **United Nations High Commission for Refugees**: 34–35 (background), 42 (all), 43 (bottom), 48, 50 (both), 51 (left), 54 (left), 59 (bottom left, top right). **United Nations Photos**: cover, 4–5, 7 (both), 8, 9, 10, 11, 12–13 (all), 15 (right), 17 (left), 18, 19 (both), 20 (all), 21 (all), 22–23, 24, 25 (both), 26, 29, 36, 38, 39, 40, 41 (left), 43 (top left and right), 44–45, 46 (artwork by Otavio Roth, reproduced by permission of Ana Beatriz Lorch Roth), 47, 49 (both), 51 (right), 52–53, 54 (right), 55 (left), 56 (both), 57, 58, 59 (top left, bottom right), 61 (all).

CONTENTS

Chapter 1

A CLUB FOR ALL COUNTRIES

What is the United Nations? Well, if you think of the world as a big neighbourhood, then the United Nations is the organization that helps everyone live together in that neighbourhood.

You probably have lots of families in your neighbourhood. Some are big, while others have only one or two people in them. Some are well off and some have a hard time making ends meet. Most of the families seem to live at peace with themselves and their neighbours. Others always seem to be fighting. But one thing almost all families have in common is pride. They don't want other people telling them how to run their lives. If these families were countries, you could call their right to manage their own affairs their sovereignty.

Of course a family's independence has limits. Everyone has to obey the law. You can't hurt people or steal. There are even laws to stop people from making a lot of noise at night. If anyone breaks the law, someone will call the police. Even within a family, police can step in to stop violence. In your neighbourhood there are probably people who help when others get sick or when a family runs out of money. There are schools and parks. As well, people elect governments to provide law, order and many other things.

The big neighbourhood

The world is the biggest neighbourhood you know. It has almost 200 countries. Some nations are huge. The nations with the most people are China, with 1.2 billion people, and India, with 883 million. The biggest in area is Russia, which covers 17 075 400 km² (6 593 328 square miles). Canada is second largest, with 9 958 319 km² (3 845 208 square miles) but only 27 million people. Some countries are tiny. One of the smallest nations, San Marino, has 23 000 people and covers only 25 km² (10 square miles).

The world is not like your neighbourhood. There isn't a world government to keep law and order. Instead, the world is like a big school yard where no one has the power to stop fights or keep gangs or bullies from hurting other kids. That's why wars and fighting and stealing have gone on forever. It was only 50 years ago, after the worst war ever, that Canada and other countries helped start the United Nations (UN). The members of the UN agreed to work together to stop wars and help each other, but still remain independent countries. In 1995 the UN had 185 member countries. A few more join every year.

For a world organization, the UN is really very small. In 1992–93, the UN budget was only $2.4 billion American. That's only about what the people of Newfoundland spent on their government that year. It would buy the Canadian navy only two new warships. Even though the UN has so little money, people want it to stop wars, feed the hungry and fight terrible diseases like AIDS.

No wonder some people call the UN a complete failure. However, in its first 50 years the UN has performed miracles. Read on and decide how well you think the UN has performed.

If you find a word that you don't understand, check the glossary on page 62 for an explanation.

Organizing the neighbourhood

If you and other people in your neighbourhood want to get something done, you begin by getting organized. Why not start a neighbourhood association? You would need to hold a meeting, or assembly, where each family would have one vote. If fighting is a problem in your area, you might choose a special peace committee. It would be smart to include the richest and most important families on the committee, because if they don't keep the peace, no one will. You could also form a committee to improve living conditions. And since there'll probably be arguments in your neighbourhood, how about a "court" to find a fair agreement?

The UN has all these organizations and many more. One is the oldest world organization still active, the International Telecommunications Union (ITU), which dates back to 1865. Another, the International Civil Aviation Organization (ICAO), has its headquarters in Montreal. It's the only UN organization with its home in Canada.

The General Assembly

Remember that "assembly" in which each family in your neighbourhood had a vote? At the UN it is called the General Assembly. Each country in the UN can have five people (called delegates) and one vote in the General Assembly. The General Assembly decides what countries can join and approves the UN budget. It makes lots of recommendations, and when UN member countries agree on something, the world listens.

The General Assembly meets in New York on the third Tuesday of each September, a day known

Boutros Boutros-Ghali (left), head of the UN, visiting the ICAO headquarters in Montreal in December 1994 to celebrate the ICAO's fiftieth anniversary

Here's the General Assembly during its forty-ninth session, in September 1994.

as Peace Day. Members choose a president of the General Assembly, 21 vice-presidents, and committees and heads of committees, making sure all regions of the world are represented. For the first few weeks there is a general debate about situations in different countries.

After this debate the General Assembly delegates spend most of their time in committees. By December the whole Assembly is ready to vote on the committees' decisions. Any decisions that are agreed on are accepted by the whole Assembly. The General Assembly breaks up in mid-December, but it is often called back to discuss an emergency or a special issue such as disarmament.

Most people at the General Assembly look like other New York office workers, though some wear their own national costumes. They spend a lot of time talking to one another outside the Assembly because, although delegates have to ask their government how they should vote, a country may have to support another country to get votes for its own cause. Chatting helps a delegate decide the best way to cast his vote.

THERÈSE PAQUET-SÉVIGNY

Thérèse Paquet-Sévigny is a journalist and professor and a world-recognized expert in communications. She was president of an advertising agency and from 1983 to 1987 she was vice-president for public relations at the Canadian Broadcasting Corporation. Then in 1987 the UN asked her to take on one of its very important jobs.

As Under-Secretary-General of the Public Information Department, Paquet-Sévigny made sure that people around the world knew what the UN was doing, not only with its projects in developing countries but also at its headquarters in New York. She had to work with many people and groups and make information available in numerous languages. Paquet-Sévigny is now a professor in the Department of Communications at the Université du Québec in Montreal.

The Security Council

The Security Council is the most important UN body after the General Assembly. Its job is to try to stop wars. Because it is so important, when it was set up in 1945, the five most powerful countries at that time (the United States, the Soviet Union, Britain, France and China) each got the right to stop, or veto, any of its decisions. This means they all have to agree before the Security Council can take action. They still have that right, and in many crises, the veto has stopped the Council from doing anything. These five countries are permanent members of the Council and the rest of the UN members take turns filling the other ten places.

That may make it seem as if the Security Council does very little, but without it things would have been worse. The fact that the world has survived without a nuclear war may be because both sides keep talking, even angrily, in the Security Council.

Anything that affects world peace may be up for discussion in the Security Council, from the capture of a fishing boat in another country's waters to working towards a ceasefire in a war zone. How does the UN work for peace? In 1945, some people thought that the UN should have its own powerful army controlled by the Security Council. Other countries didn't like the idea – what if the UN's army was sent to fight them? So, instead of having its own army, when the UN wants to punish a country, as in the Gulf War of 1990 (page 33), or when it tries to keep peace, such as in the Bosnia situation (page 33), it must persuade member countries to lend their soldiers and sometimes also to pay their costs. When soldiers are being killed, it's hard to find volunteers!

The Security Council's many duties include choosing the Secretary-General and recommending new members to the General Assembly.

Canada was elected to the Security
Council in 1948–49, 1958–59,
1967–68, 1977–78 and 1989–90.

The Secretary-General

The Secretary-General is the UN's top boss. Almost 27 000 people work for him, in many different jobs ranging from heads of international organizations to security guards. He also commands as many as 50 000 soldiers lent by members for peacekeeping duties.

The Secretary-General is appointed by the General Assembly on the recommendation of the Security Council. That means that the great powers have to agree on one person and that person immediately becomes very powerful.

The Secretary-General's biggest job is to manage many organizations and thousands of staff members. The staff comes from all over the world and must give up national loyalties to serve the world. Sometimes they must live in foreign countries in harsh conditions. The Secretary-General must make sure that both men and women, as well as all the various countries, religions and races, are well represented at the UN. The Secretary-General has one of the most important jobs in the world, and one of the toughest.

Boutros Boutros-Ghali is the sixth Secretary-General and he's held the position since 1992. The world must seem like a rather small neighbourhood to him. He was born in Egypt (where his father was prime minister) in 1922 but was educated in France and the United States and he speaks three languages fluently. It is important that Boutros-Ghali comes from a country at the northeast corner of Africa since there has never been an African Secretary-General before. So far his biggest accomplishment as Secretary-General has been to get UN members to pay the dues they owe. He has also had to cope with tragedies such as the situations in Bosnia and Rwanda.

**Boutros Boutros-Ghali (right) meeting
with the Foreign Minister of Canada,
André Ouellet, in November 1993**

The Economic and Social Council

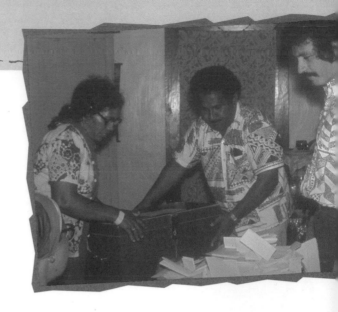

If preventing war is the UN's biggest problem, helping the world's people live peacefully is part of the solution. That's the aim of the UN's Economic and Social Council (ECOSOC). It discusses issues such as health, education and world trade. Its 53 members are elected by the General Assembly and they meet twice a year, once in New York City and once in Geneva, Switzerland.

Five Regional Economic Commissions report to ECOSOC, one commission each for Europe, Asia and the Pacific, Latin America, Africa and Western Asia. They try to persuade their countries to solve economic problems together. Other commissions specialize in global issues, including human rights and drug abuse.

The Trusteeship Council

The Trusteeship Council ensured that colonies are treated fairly. The UN has worked towards making colonies independent countries, and by 1985 only one small "trust" remained, a scattering of tiny islands in the Pacific Ocean.

The International Court of Justice

Remember how you thought about giving your neighbourhood a place where people could settle arguments? Countries can take their disputes to the International Court of Justice, but they must agree in advance to respect its judgement. A Canadian, John Read, helped draw up the rules for the court and from 1946 to 1958 served as a judge. The 15 judges of the International Court are nominated by the Security Council and approved by the General Assembly. They come from all parts of the world and various legal systems – can you imagine how difficult it must be for them to work together?

There are lots of disagreements in the world, but the International Court has made fewer than 50 judgements. That's because few countries want to put important issues before 15 foreign judges, though most judges have good records of ignoring their national loyalties.

UN workers helping with the voting process
that will lead to independence for the island
of Niue in the South Pacific Ocean

Lots of committees

In half a century the UN has added many committees, programs and organizations. In 1994 more than 50 committees and working groups reported to the Assembly. These ranged from the United Nations Economic, Social and Cultural Organization (UNESCO) in Paris to the International Research and Training Institute for the Advancement of Women (INSTRAW) in the Dominican Republic.

Most agencies specialize in particular issues, for example health (the World Health Organization), workers and working conditions (the International Labour Organization) and ocean shipping (the International Maritime Organization or IMO). Some are highly technical, such as the World Meteorological Organization (WMO), which helps collect weather information. Helping developing nations creates a lot of new organizations, such as the United Nations Industrial Development Organization (UNIDO), which tries to help manufacturing industries in the developing countries, and the International Fund for Agricultural Development (IFAD), which lends money for agriculture.

New organizations can also result from UN conferences. The UN Environment Program (UNEP) was a result of a 1972 conference in Stockholm. The World Food Council (WFC) was an answer to a food crisis in the 1970s. Wars around the world have left the UN with more than a dozen special commissions, usually headed by a general from one of the member nations who then is commander of the peacekeeping forces.

The UN's vast family of organizations is very complicated – but not nearly as complicated as the world it is trying to help!

When the people of the Sahelian Zone of West Africa were facing famine in 1973 due to drought, the UN Food and Agriculture Organization (FAO) provided food.

The United Nations Headquarters

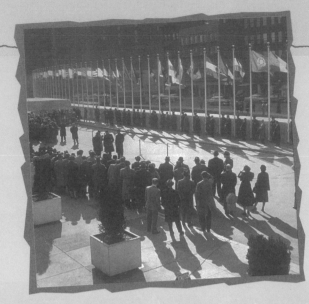

The flags of all the countries th are members of the UN fly in UN Plaza.

The United Nations Headquarters covers 7.3 ha (18 acres) or about 6 blocks in New York City. It consists of the 39-storey tall Secretariat building, the domed General Assembly Hall, the Conference Building which connects them, and the Dag Hammarskjöld Library. Canadian architect Ernest Cormier was a member of the group that helped design the headquarters. Canada donated wood and seven beautifully decorated metal doors to the buildings.

The main visitors' entrance is at the north end of the General Assembly building. Over 1500 people visit the headquarters daily.

The Security Council Chamber is beside the Trusteeship Council Chamber in the Conference Building.

The General Assembly Hall is seven storeys high and seats over 2100 delegates. Each seat is equipped with earphones through which the delegates can hear translations of all speeches given. Speeches are translated into Arabic, Chinese, English, French, Russian and Spanish, the six official languages of the General Assembly.

Chapter 2

Birth of the United Nations

In your neighbourhood and even in your home, you take it for granted that people need some way to keep order, settle fights and, if possible, keep bullies from beating up other people. Most countries would like that, too.

In 1914 many people believed that war, at least a war that would involve most of Europe, was almost impossible. Nations had so many better ways to settle their arguments, and if there was a war, they would lose too much. Yet when World War I began in August, within days all the big countries of Europe were involved. Since Canada was a British colony, Canada was at war, too. When the war ended in 1918, winners and losers had all lost millions of lives and most of their wealth.

The League of Nations

Part of the peace settlement after World War I was a plan for an organization called the League of Nations. It would unite countries to help keep peace, settle disputes and tackle injustices that might lead to new wars.

Canada was eager to join the League of Nations. The war had cost it 60 000 soldiers and a lot of money. As well, Canadians no longer wanted to be a colony. Belonging to the League of Nations was a good way to tell the world that from then on Canada would speak for itself.

Problems, problems

You might think that all countries would support an organization working for world peace. It wasn't that simple. Americans, for example, felt that having Canada and Australia in the League added to Britain's influence. Since Canada and Australia had been colonies of Britain, Americans assumed that they would vote the same way as Britain.

The United States also didn't like one part of the League's rules that said members had to go to war to defend the peace treaty. Americans didn't want anyone telling them they had to fight. Neither did Canada, but it stayed in the League. The Americans stayed out. That left too much responsibility for the League with Britain and France. When the Germans, who had lost the war to the British allies, joined the League, they did not feel welcome.

Another problem was that the League had been set up so that it could make decisions only when all members agreed. The League was helpless when countries drifted into a new world war. For Canada, World War II began on September 10, 1939. The United States became involved on December 7, 1941, when Japan attacked Hawaii.

BROCK CHISHOLM

Dr. Brock Chisholm became the first Canadian to play a major role in the UN when he was made the first Director-General of the World Health Organization (WHO). He'd already headed many important groups. He'd been the head of the Canadian army's medical services in World War II, and generals learned then that he was outspoken. They usually took his advice. After the war, in 1945, Chisholm became Canada's deputy minister of health – and he was still outspoken.

Chisholm began work as head of WHO in 1948. He organized a worldwide attack on malaria and tuberculosis and he insisted that mothers and children get top priority in WHO programs. And he was still outspoken, attacking aid programs that gave showy results but little long-term change. Fifty years ago, he already saw the dangers of pollution, overpopulation and nuclear weapons. And he spoke out about them!

New hope

Less than a month after the United States entered World War II, US President Franklin Delano Roosevelt used the words "United Nations" to describe the 26 nations working together against Japan and Germany. Soon the words described the forces that worked together to slowly push back the Germans in Europe, led by Adolf Hitler, and the Japanese in the Pacific. When allied leaders got together during the war, they often discussed a new United Nations organization.

The big allied countries had the most to say about the new organization. From August to October in 1944, representatives of the United States, Great Britain, China and the Union of Soviet Socialist Republics (USSR) met at Dumbarton Oaks, just outside Washington, DC,

to plan the UN. Instead of saving the old League of Nations, they decided to start again. Like the League, the new UN would have an Assembly with equal voice for all countries. It would also have a Security Council, a smaller council to make decisions on world peace and security. Instead of requiring all countries to agree, only two-thirds of the Assembly members had to approve a resolution. However, the four powers at Dumbarton Oaks, plus France, would be permanent members of the Council and each of them would have the right to prevent, or veto, any decision they opposed.

Many countries complained about the special privileges given to the great powers. Shouldn't all nations be equal? That sounds good but it didn't fit the facts. The success of the UN depended on its most powerful members. If a great power got really angry, it would probably walk out. Everyone remembered how not having the United States in the League of Nations had weakened it. In 1945, it was

Canadians were an important part of the Allied forces in World War II. These Canadian soldiers are marching through a German town.

Delegates discussing a new organization
for peace at Dumbarton Oaks
in August 1944

mainly the Soviet Union that feared
isolation and wanted the right to a veto. But
eventually, Great Britain, France, China and
even the United States would also use the veto.

Why wasn't Canada a great power? It had
the third-largest navy in the world and the
fourth-largest air force, and a big share in
developing the atomic bomb. But Canada's big
allies didn't want to share their power, nor did
Canada's Prime Minister William Lyon
Mackenzie King want all the problems that
come with power. So during the war King left
the big decisions to American and British
leaders, and he was not upset that Canada was
left out of the talks at Dumbarton Oaks. Instead,
Canada's ambassador to the United States,
Lester B. Pearson (see page 25), worked hard
to make the Americans see the importance of
the UN and to encourage them to become a
member.

YVONNE KUPSCH

The UN first became a part of Yvonne Kupsch's life
during International Youth Year in 1985. She was
working for a youth volunteer program in Saskatoon,
Saskatchewan, that did many things, including
involving young people in tree planting as a way
of finding out more about the environment. Soon
she was at UN headquarters in New York on a
committee of the Tree Project. This project supports
tree planting all over the world.

In 1986, Vancouver's UN Association sent
Kupsch to Africa as part of a program called Trees
for Africa. She returned to Canada convinced that
Canadians must work as partners with African
people. Kupsch's work helps not only poor people in
Africa but also people around the world. Since trees
are natural air filters, planting them gives us all
more and better air to breathe.

The miracle at San Francisco

One way to help the Americans overcome their suspicions of the UN was to have the UN's birthplace in the United States. On April 15, 1945, the founding meeting for the new organization opened in San Francisco, California. It lasted two months and negotiations were extremely difficult. The Americans and the Soviets were both suspicious of an organization that could be more powerful than either one of them. As well, smaller countries wanted equality with the great powers, and their anger over not receiving it could well have broken up the conference.

Canada's Lester Pearson and the other Canadian diplomats had orders from Prime Minister Mackenzie King to make sure that the British, the Soviets and especially the Americans stayed in the new organization. Otherwise, King knew, it would fail.

Somehow, a miracle happened at San Francisco. The fact that the war in Europe ended on May 5, 1945, while negotiations were going on, helped, since all the countries realized that they would have to work together to face the postwar world. The big powers stayed in the UN and the smaller countries felt they would be heard in the General Assembly. ECOSOC and the Trusteeship Council (see page 10) were designed to reassure them. Compromises were found, sometimes by Canadians. That would often be Canada's UN role in the future – and the headlines would go to others. But already in 1945 Canada had a great name at the UN, thanks to the country's many

William Lyon Mackenzie King, Canada's prime minister, signing the Charter of the United Nations on June 26, 1945

The first session of the UN General Assembly took place on September 10, 1946, in London, England.

outstanding diplomats, including Lester Pearson, Jules Léger and Norman Robertson.

At the end of the conference, on June 26, 1945, all 46 of the national delegations present signed the new agreement, the Charter of the United Nations. (You can read its opening words on page 60.) Final approval, of course, depended on their governments. By October 24, 1945, there were 31 governments that had agreed to the Charter. By the end of the year, the organization had more than 50 members. Thus the United Nations was born and ever since, October 24 has been the official United Nations Day.

MAURICE STRONG

Maurice Strong has had many occupations, including businessman, senior civil servant and expert on foreign aid. But ever since he was 18, he has always found time to work where his heart is – for the UN. Thirty years ago, Strong realized that saving the world environment had to become a UN issue. And it couldn't just be a concern for rich countries. Poor countries, desperate to feed their people, often do the worst things to their environments. In 1972, Strong helped lead the Stockholm Conference on the environment. Then he became first head of the United Nations Environmental Program (UNEP). Twenty years later, Strong was also the person behind the UN's 1992 Rio de Janeiro Conference on the environment. In between, the UN asked him to organize famine relief in Africa after the terrible droughts of the 1980s. Strong is one Canadian who has definitely made a difference.

Getting organized

When the UN was created, much of Europe and Asia lay in ruins. People were starving. Millions, uprooted from their homes by the war, were labelled Displaced Persons or DPs and crowded into camps. Even before the UN was officially formed, an agency called the United Nations Relief and Rehabilitation Agency tried to help them.

Like the DPs, the UN had no home. The members considered moving into the League of Nations palace in Geneva. After all, most UN members in 1945 were European. But what about keeping the Americans involved? The US Congress helped settle the issue; it invited the UN to locate its headquarters in New York City. The wealthy Rockefeller family paid for the ground and the city prepared the site. By 1952 the UN had its new home.

And what a home! There is a 39-storey office building for the Secretary-General and the UN staff (called the Secretariat), halls where the councils meet, and the vast General Assembly Hall. In 1961, the Dag Hammarskjöld Library (named after the UN's second Secretary-General) was completed (you can see all these buildings on pages 12–13). The UN also chose its symbol: a map of the world as seen from the North Pole, surrounded by a wreath of olive branches, the symbol of peace.

The UN also needed its own staff to carry out the work of the General Assembly and the other councils. How good the staff would be depended on its top official, the Secretary-General. The great powers, already at odds on so many issues, could not agree on who should get the job. One of the most popular candidates was Canada's Lester Pearson. But if the UN was to be in the United States, should it have a North American as its top official? The compromise was to choose Trygve Lie, a Norwegian lawyer and politician who had once been very friendly with the Soviet Union.

Two of the millions of displaced persons in Europe. These DPs fled from Ukraine.

Nikita Khrushchev, prime minister of the former Soviet Union, was a major leader in the Cold War.

The Cold War

The UN got to work. First, a place had to be found for valuable international organizations left over from the League of Nations. The International Court that met at The Hague in Holland was renamed the World Court and its judges continued to hear international disputes. The International Labour Organization (ILO), World Meteorological Organization (WMO) and International Postal Union (IPU) went right on working.

New organizations were needed, too. To help feed a starving postwar world, a Food and Agriculture Organization (FAO) took shape in Rome. In 1948, the World Health Organization (WHO) began with a Canadian, Dr. Brock Chisholm, as its first Director-General (see page 15). The World Bank and the International Monetary Fund (IMF) were created in Washington, the capital of the world's richest country, to help European countries rebuild their ruined economies. The Soviet Union and its bloc of allies refused to join the IMF. Already the UN had problems.

The UN had other tough issues to work on. The Soviet government believed in communism, the idea that, after a world revolution, everyone would be equal and share the world's wealth. This was an exciting idea, especially for people in poor countries, but meanwhile the Soviet Union was enforcing communism by using violence. As the world's richest country, the United States opposed communism and said that it was just an excuse for the Soviet Union to spread its power. Smaller countries lined up on either side or tried to stay out of what might become a third world war. Naturally, the UN became a noisy battleground in what many people called the Cold War. It was called that because it wasn't quite hot enough to be a real war, but it seemed ready to become one at any time. Keeping the Cold War from turning hot would be the UN's single biggest job.

Here are the logos of some of the many UN organizations.

Chapter 3

KEEPING THE PEACE

Remember that neighbourhood association you decided to form back in Chapter 1? You also decided that it should have a committee to stop any fights. But sometimes even the committee can't do much. There was that time when the two richest families spent a fortune trying to out-do each other. It ended after one family ran out of money. Even the poorer families spend more time and money than they can afford quarrelling. And when any families get into a fight, the other families are afraid of getting hurt if they try to stop it.

So what can your neighbourhood association do? When trouble is brewing, the head of the peace committee tries to talk to both sides. Sometimes talking to a good listener can cool off anger. But once two sides have started to fight, all the committee can do is keep others from joining in, and separate the sides when it can. It might be better to have special laws, and neighbourhood police to make people obey the laws, but that's not how neighbourhoods are set up. And the world doesn't work that way either.

After the war

Stopping the end of the world

The UN was begun during World War II, the worst war ever. While the delegates met at San Francisco, the atomic bomb was being tested. Six weeks later, at Hiroshima and Nagasaki in Japan, these horrible bombs killed 150 000 men, women and children. Thousands more died later from radiation sickness, something no one had expected. It was clear to everyone that another world war could wipe out everyone on Earth. Yet instead of agreeing to get rid of their weapons, the UN's great powers – the United States, the Soviet Union and their allies – began making new and more terrible bombs and building huge armies, navies and air forces. What had gone wrong?

After World War II, the United States was rich enough to spend lots of money rebuilding Europe and helping its friends. The Soviet Union had been devastated by the war – people were starving, cities and towns had been flattened and farms had been ruined. The Soviets were afraid their neighbours might take advantage of these weaknesses, so they decided to move first. They used their army to control Poland, Romania, Bulgaria and Hungary, and in 1948 they took over Czechoslovakia.

Even though the Soviet Union was weak, it was obviously on the attack. That scared Britain, France and other European countries, who banded together and asked the United States and Canada for help. In 1949 the two North American and ten European countries created the North Atlantic Treaty Organization (NATO). This made the Soviet Union uneasy and the Cold War (page 21) became warmer.

The UN as battleground

Throughout the 1950s, the Cold War between East (the Soviet Union and allies) and West (the United States and allies) affected almost every UN decision. East-West battles filled Canadian Lester Pearson's year as President of the General Assembly in 1952. Secretary-General Trygve Lie's term ended because he had angered the Soviets and discussions came to a deadlock. His successor, Dag Hammarskjöld, came from Sweden, a country that tried to be neutral.

UN membership was open to "peace-loving states which accept the obligations contained in the present Charter and, in the judgement of the Organization, are able and willing to carry out these obligations." However, when new countries tried to join, Soviet countries voted against countries likely to back the United States, and the Americans and their friends voted to keep out Soviet allies. In 1955, Paul Martin, leading Canada's delegation, patiently persuaded the Americans and the Soviets to allow in 16 countries that supported either side or none. Thanks to

Martin's work, almost any country could join the UN after 1955 (except for China, which the United States blocked until 1972 because it was a communist country).

Even when the UN did act, it got into trouble. In 1960, when the UN became involved in peacekeeping in the Congo in Africa, that country's government insisted that the UN send in its soldiers to end a rebellion in the country. Out of respect for the Congo government, Secretary-General Hammarskjöld agreed. The result was more killing and chaos. When the Congo's prime minister was killed, his friends blamed the UN for not rescuing him. Then some UN members wondered why they were in the Congo at all and refused to pay their share of UN costs.

Almost 15 000 soldiers from ten countries served with the UN force in Leopoldville in the Congo.

In 1961, Hammarskjöld died in a plane crash in Africa. His assistant, U Thant from Burma, took over. He and the Secretaries-General who came after him were more cautious about taking on dangerous and difficult tasks. They had to be. The Congo operation had left the UN with a huge debt. When the UN took on peacekeeping tasks in Cyprus in 1964, in Egypt, Lebanon and Syria after the 1973 Arab-Israeli War, and in Central America and Africa later, it was careful to make sure that their forces were welcome and their way would be paid.

LESTER B. PEARSON

You may know about Lester Pearson as a prime minister, but long before he became Canada's fourteenth PM he was working for the UN. He was one of Canada's representatives at the conference in San Francisco when the UN was founded. As Canada's secretary of state for external affairs, Pearson helped lead Canada into the Korean War (see page 33) as a member of the UN army. In 1952–53 he served as President of the United Nations General Assembly as well as Chairman of the NATO Council. And one of the most important things Pearson did was to come up with the plan to end the Suez Crisis in 1956 (see page 32). Because of his work to end this crisis he won the Nobel Peace Prize in 1957, making him the only individual Canadian ever to earn this honour.

Canadian soldiers fighting for the UN in Korea in 1951 faced great hardships and received many injuries.

The struggle against war

What can the UN do for peace? Through decisions and resolutions in the General Assembly, it tells the world that war is the wrong way to settle arguments. It pleads with its members to limit the number of weapons they have, especially nuclear weapons. It sends the Secretary-General to countries in conflict in order to help opponents reach peaceful agreements. It writes laws for using the ocean and outer space. The UN pressured South Africa to end cruel policies that could only lead to all-out war between its black and white people.

When a war breaks out between members, the Security Council reminds one or both sides that they have broken their commitment to the UN's Charter. Sometimes the UN can get both sides to stop fighting in a few days. Then the UN can send in observers or peacekeeping troops to separate the warring sides and make sure the fighting doesn't begin again. It can also send in food and medicine for the victims. The UN usually cannot intervene in a civil war, a war in which people of the same country fight each other, but it can prevent other countries from helping either side by sending arms and soldiers.

A Canadian soldier showing landmines that the UN Protection Force has found in Croatia

Canadian soldiers serving with the UN in Rwanda have had many jobs.

The UN has three weapons in the struggle against war:

+ It encourages members to disarm.

+ It supports a world court and new laws to settle arguments.

+ It borrow soldiers from its members to keep the peace and, if necessary, to fight for it.

CANADIAN PEACEKEEPERS

Between 1947 and 1994, more than 120 000 Canadians have served as peacekeepers in every UN operation. It can be very dangerous work. On June 19, 1994, Corporal Mark Isfeld became the hundredth Canadian peacekeeper to die on duty since 1950. Isfeld died in Croatia when he was clearing explosive landmines to make an area safe for others.

Peacekeeping takes great courage, and in 1988 Canadian soldiers shared the honour with soldiers around the world of winning the Nobel Peace Prize. Peacekeeping soldiers may be called on to do many tasks. Canadian soldiers stand guard on ceasefire lines or provide communications. Pilots fly in dangerous conditions to provide UN workers with food and medical supplies. Members of the Royal Canadian Mounted Police and other police forces help supervise UN-sponsored elections.

Canadian UN troops in the former Yugoslavia

Disarmament

One of the first things the UN did when it was started was try to get its members to disarm or destroy all their weapons. But neither the East nor the West felt safe enough to do so. There were many discussions about disarmament, sometimes just between the United States and the Soviet Union, and sometimes involving other countries. However, by talking about all the ways the other side might cheat, disarmament talks may have increased fears. Canadian experts helped by working hard to find ways to check on each side's progress without raising suspicions of spying.

And sometimes there was progress. The UN organized an agreement to ban poison gas and weapons that carry the germs of horrible diseases. Most countries agreed never to test nuclear bombs in the open air (they still tested them in caves or underground).

The arms race did finally end in the 1990s, but UN members couldn't take much credit for stopping it. What really ended it was that the cost of arms made countries go broke. In 1989, the Soviet bloc collapsed. Most of the republics in the old Soviet Union announced their independence. The Cold War was over.

You'd think countries would have learned their lesson. But Soviet countries now desperate for money sold their weapons and technology to other countries at bargain rates. The dream of world disarmament remained a dream and the world needed the UN more than ever.

World law

Another way the UN tries to keep peace is by making international laws, fair laws that apply to all countries. The idea of world law dates back almost to the time of Christopher Columbus. Since then, countries have accepted many rules of international law. In 1948 the UN's new

These surface-to-surface missiles are just
a few of the arms held by the Soviets
before the end of the Cold War.

International Law Commission (ILC) made laws concerning the Holocaust, the mass murder of 6 million Jews during World War II. The ILC made it a crime called genocide to attempt to destroy a race or entire group of people. At Vienna in 1961, an ILC conference agreed on how ambassadors and their staffs would be treated by host countries. The ILC also wrote rules to protect people who have no country. Other new laws deal with outer space and with the mineral wealth under the oceans.

Like most decisions the UN and its committees have to make, international laws are difficult to agree on. For example, should only countries with shores along the ocean own the rich minerals under the sea? What about poor countries with no ocean coast? As well, countries with a space program have very different ideas about who should control outer space than do countries that can never even afford a seat on a space shuttle.

As for taking disputes to the International Court of Justice (page 10), most countries still refuse.

THE NANSEN MEDAL

The United Nations High Commission for Refugees (UNHCR) gives the Nansen Medal to people or organizations especially helpful to refugees. Canada is the only country ever to win this award. The medal is named in honour of Norwegian explorer Fridtjof Nansen. He gave his time and money to help people forced to flee their countries because of war and political fights. Usually these refugees did not have passports or identity cards, but Nansen persuaded countries to recognize the "Nansen Passport," a special card for refugees.

On November 13, 1986, Governor General Jeanne Sauvé accepted the Nansen Medal on behalf of all Canadians. The medal acknowledges Canada's hospitality to homeless refugees. Canada is also known around the world for recognizing the particular plight of refugee women as they try to care for themselves and their children.

Soldiers and peacekeeping

All over the world, soldiers in the UN's blue helmets or caps have risked their lives trying to stop wars. In 1988 they received one of the world's highest honours, the Nobel Peace Prize. Canadians were especially proud, because their soldiers and aircrew had shared in almost every UN peacekeeping operation since 1948.

What do peacekeepers do? Why do they have to be soldiers? Often, after two sides stop fighting and agree to a truce, each side fears that the other is cheating. Peacekeeping soldiers can see what is happening with a soldier's eye and report the truth. Canadians have been involved with UN peacekeeping in Israel, Lebanon, Yemen, Nicaragua and Cambodia. (You can read about some of these and others on pages 32–33.)

Another thing UN peacekeepers do is guard the line between warring sides. That's what Canada's Lieutenant General E.L.M. Burns organized between Egypt and Israel in 1956. In Cyprus in 1964, Canadian soldiers helped guard a "Green Line" between Turks and Greeks.

Back in 1990, UN soldiers in Nicaragua made it safe for soldiers of one side to give up their weapons without fear of being massacred. UN peacekeepers in Namibia in 1991 and in Cambodia in 1992–93 guarded voting places from attack by the side that expected to lose. Since 1992 in the former Yugoslavia, UN soldiers tried to keep people from killing one another because of ancient hatreds. In Bosnia they guarded supplies sent by the world to help people survive the war and the bitter weather.

Canadian soldiers on patrol
in Cyprus in 1967

Trying to make peace

In Korea in 1950, Iraq in 1990 and Somalia in 1993 the UN tried to make peace rather than simply keep it. When negotiations, threats, boycotts and blockades don't work, the UN can fight. But peacekeeping and peacemaking are difficult and expensive. Nothing else the UN does keeps it more in debt.

Sometimes the UN itself makes a hard job worse. Sometimes, because its members cannot make up their minds, the Security Council gives vague orders. Or its members refuse to send enough soldiers to carry out the orders.

Of 27 peacekeeping operations since 1945, very few have led to lasting peace. UN members and people around the world may ask themselves if trying to stop the killing is worth it. But doing nothing is worse.

ROMÉO DALLAIRE

A quiet soldier from Quebec, Major General Roméo Dallaire didn't expect to make history when the UN asked him to command its peacekeepers in Rwanda in 1983. But suddenly he found that there was no peace to keep. Rwandans began killing one another, as well as torturing and killing UN soldiers. The UN ordered most of its soldiers to leave Rwanda, but Dallaire, some of his staff, and soldiers from Ghana stayed, despite the fighting and killing all around them. They saved anyone they could and waited until peace returned. Whatever the risks, Dallaire kept trying to get food and medicine to suffering people. It was a desperately dangerous job, but like other Canadian peacekeepers, he accepted the challenge.

Places where the UN has worked for peace

PALESTINE

After 6 million Jews died in World War II, many UN members wanted to give Jews their own country, Israel, in Palestine. The Arabs who already lived there saw no reason why a horrible crime in Europe should cost them their homes. However, it was agreed at the UN that Palestine be directed to give Jews a home. War then broke out between Israel and its Arab neighbours as the Palestinians looked for places to live. After much work, the UN was able to arrange a truce and send in military officers, including Canadians, to help both sides stop fighting. The UN also built camps for Palestinians driven from their homes. Israel and its Arab neighbours have fought four wars since 1949, and many Canadians have served in peacekeeping forces on Israel's borders.

CYPRUS

When Britain gave up its island colony of Cyprus in the western Mediterranean, fighting soon broke out between the Greeks and Turks who lived there. Greece and Turkey seemed likely to join the fighting, so the UN agreed to send a peacekeeping force, including several hundred Canadians. War broke out again in 1973 when Greeks tried to take over the island and a Turkish army invaded, but again the UN helped establish peace. In 1993, Canada announced that it would withdraw its forces to encourage the two sides to make peace.

THE SUEZ

Israel had even more problems than its wars between the Palestinians and Arabs. For years it had been attacked by fighters from Egypt and it finally struck back in 1956. At the same time, France and Britain were angry that Egyptians had taken over the Suez Canal and they attacked too. Canada's chief UN delegate, Lester Pearson, was given the job of making peace — fast. With the help of Canada's Lieutenant General E.L.M. Burns, he brought in a force of UN soldiers from countries not involved in the war. Canadian soldiers provided communications, a hospital and many other services the UN's first army needed.

BOSNIA/CROATIA

When Yugoslavia broke up in 1991, Serbs and Croats who lived in the north began fighting for control of the land. The UN sent in a large army to stop the fighting. Then Serbs, Croats and Moslems from neighbouring Bosnia began fighting for territory far to the south at Sarajevo in Bosnia-Herzogovina. Again the UN tried to stop the killing and to protect food and fuel sent to the hungry, freezing people. Two Canadian regiments were part of the UN force and Major General Lewis Mackenzie, a Canadian soldier, was one of the leaders of the group trying to stop the fighting at Sarajevo.

KOREA

On June 25, 1950, Communist-controlled North Korea attacked South Korea. The United States demanded that the UN stop the attack. The Soviet delegates, who were also Communists, had already walked out of the UN because the Americans and their allies would not let communist China join the UN. That meant the Soviets weren't on hand to say no to the American demands. So the UN told the United States to stop North Korea. During the war China sent volunteers to help North Korea and there was bitter fighting. Canada sent soldiers, warships and transport planes, as did 15 other UN members. Many soldiers were killed before the Korean War ended on July 27, 1953. The UN saved South Korea but the war did not punish the invaders.

IRAQ/KUWAIT

In August 1990, Iraq's leader, Saddam Hussein, sent his army to conquer neighbouring Kuwait. When UN threats and boycotts failed to make him withdraw his army, the United States organized a UN force, including Canadians, to protect Iraq's other neighbours and, in January 1991, to free Kuwait. The allied countries won back Kuwait, but Saddam Hussein was still in power and his armies wrecked the little country.

CAMBODIA

Cambodia is a country that has been torn apart by internal wars for many years. To help bring peace, in 1992–93 the UN organized an election to help Cambodians choose their next government. Canadians were part of the UN force, mostly from Asian countries, that was on hand to prevent the election from being destroyed by one of the warring groups.

Chapter 4

SERVING THE DEVELOPING NATIONS

Last month your neighbourhood association had a really big problem to deal with. It involved two families — a family in which both parents had lost their jobs and the richest family on the block. People began taking sides and soon almost everyone in the neighbourhood was fighting.

Just as in your neighbourhood, the gap between rich and poor people in the world is a much larger threat to peace than nuclear weapons and deadly gases. The poor have always fought for a share of wealth, but sometimes rich people don't share until they're forced to or unless they're afraid they'll have everything taken from them.

More than fear should make people and countries share the world's wealth. There are few deaths more agonizing than starvation. None is more unnecessary, since the world has food and clean water for everyone. As well, when most children don't get an education, the world loses the brain power it needs to solve problems and improve everyone's living conditions.

"Poor" or "developing"?

Nobody wants to be called poor. Neither do countries. The word "developing" is probably a better word to describe these countries. After all, if you could go back in time a few hundred years and visit what are now some of the richest countries in the world, you would have called them poor. Most people were badly fed, the poor wore rags, the few roads were impassable and bands of robbers roamed the countryside. Even the wealthiest people were cold in winter, lacked basic health care and lived in filthy conditions. Over a few hundred years, those countries developed. So will countries we now call "less developed."

Today's developed countries often made progress because they took resources from less-developed countries. Every day you use porcelain from China, cotton cloth from India or potatoes from South America. Maybe it's time for developed countries to pay back less-developed countries.

MARGARET CATLEY-CARLSON

The most important skills Margaret Catley-Carlson brought to the UN were her abilities to organize and manage. She was a Canadian diplomat and an expert on international aid. Catley-Carlson worked for the Canadian International Development Agency (CIDA), then in 1981 Ottawa sent her to work with the United Nations Children's Fund (UNICEF). It was an interesting time to be there because UNICEF was changing its priorities from fighting hunger to promoting health and from focusing on Asia to working in Africa. Catley-Carlson became an Assistant Under-Secretary at the UN and Deputy Executive-Director at UNICEF. She did her work so well that Prime Minister Trudeau put her in charge of CIDA in 1983. She ran CIDA until 1989, when she became deputy minister of the Department of Health and Welfare.

Colonies grow up

How do you feel when someone tells you what you should do and think? You probably don't like it. In 1952 the General Assembly agreed that it was important for countries to make their own decisions and be independent. It required countries to help their colonies stand on their own, the process known as decolonization.

As colonies became independent and joined the UN, they demanded faster decolonization. Between 1955 and 1970, of the 64 new members who joined, 54 had been colonies. By 1970, most of the 124 UN members had once been colonies.

Most developing countries were poor and eager for the UN's help. Not surprisingly, they often had a very different view of the world from long-time UN members. And since each country in the General Assembly had one vote, a tiny former colony with barely enough money to send a delegate to New York had the same voice as the United States.

Developing countries also insisted on being part of UN councils and committees. In 1965, the Security Council grew from 11 to 15 members. The Economic and Social Council grew from 27 members in 1965 to 54 in 1973. The World Bank and the International Monetary Fund had to make room for the UN's new members, too. The World Bank tried to solve new members' problems with special funds and banks that specialized in African and Caribbean concerns.

The UN's own staff also changed, since member countries were each promised a number of jobs for their own people. By the 1980s the UN staff had grown to 25 000 people.

Challenging white power

Developing countries brought more to the UN than a desire to be involved in committees. Many countries disliked the way white South Africans held all the power in the country even though many more blacks lived there.

General Assembly President Amara Essy met with Nelson Mandela in October 1994.

South Africa's policy of discrimination (called *apartheid*) kept whites and blacks apart. Its police enforced the rules harshly and locked up anyone who protested. Although the UN is not allowed to interfere in a member's affairs, it did cancel South Africa's membership and made a big effort to stop trading with it. Finally in 1993 blacks gained the right to vote and share power with whites. In 1994 Nelson Mandela was elected president of South Africa, and the country became a UN member again.

White power was challenged in other African countries. The UN voted to make Namibia, a colony of South Africa since 1919, independent in 1966. Independence finally came in 1991 after much fighting. In 1965, troubles began in Rhodesia, a British colony, when the white minority declared its independence so it wouldn't have to share power with the black majority. The General Assembly ordered the British to crush the uprising. It took 15 years of fighting for black Rhodesians to win their new country. They renamed it Zimbabwe and joined the UN in 1980.

JEAN STECKLE

Jean Steckle grew up on a farm in Kitchener, Ontario, and her interest in farming took her around the world. In 1958 she joined the United Nations Food and Agriculture Organization (FAO) and spent much of the next 12 years in Ghana and Sierra Leone in Africa helping to battle malnourishment.

Steckle then joined the International Development Research Centre based in Ottawa. The focus of the Centre is to assist developing countries with problems that the country wants help with. The Centre provides expertise and training as well as money. Experts today continue the work Steckle was involved with by meeting with experts from developing countries to discover what goals the people of the country have and then helping them achieve their goals.

Decades of development

Helping new countries develop is as important as helping them become independent. The UN's Charter requires the UN to "promote higher standards of living, full employment and conditions of social progress and development." What was the point of being independent if a country was too poor to feed, educate or care for its people?

The UN had little power or money to bring much help to developing countries. What it could do was make the issues concerning trade, population, women and the environment known through conferences. Through agreements and resolutions, it tried to commit richer countries

such as the United States and Canada to do their share. In the 1960s and 1970s the UN started agencies to promote low-cost housing; protection of the environment; sharing technical knowledge, especially with women; and many other solutions to development problems.

The United Nations Development Program (UNDP), created in 1965 to unite smaller organizations, became the world's biggest agency for giving expert assistance. Financed by voluntary contributions from UN members, the UN's development fund now spends about $1.2 billion on 5900 projects. It sends experts and managers to help developing countries and it sends thousands of people from those countries to learn abroad. The UNDP has delivered all kinds of equipment, from shovels to computers. It has persuaded governments and companies to invest more than $100 billion in its projects. Since 1960, the great number of developing countries helped make the UN into the world's biggest organization for international development. The 1960s were declared the Decade of Development.

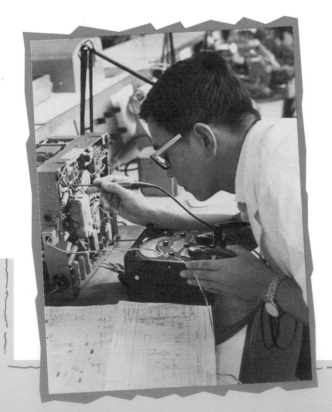

The UNDP and the International Telecommunications Union (ITU) helped set up this telecommunications training centre in Kuala Lumpur, Malaysia.

Living with 5 billion people

Organizations created to rebuild war-ravaged Europe adapted, and UN agencies were started, to help starving people.

What else can the UN do for developing countries? Through its member nations, the UN can supply every kind of knowledge, from weather forecasting to telecommunications. The UN has recruited experts to design airports and to choose trees that can replace vanished forests. Canada's ambassador to the UN from 1984 to 1988, Stephen Lewis, was a strong supporter of more aid to Africa. In 1986 he was named a UN special advisor on African affairs.

The UN has organized studies on how to stop deserts from spreading and how better fishing and food-packing methods improve health. International and regional conferences discuss problems ranging from the global environment to sharing the Jordan River's water supply. The biggest problem the UN's environmental programs face is trying to persuade countries, many of them very poor, to worry about tomorrow, not today.

Ever heard of Matej Gaspar? He was born in Zagreb, Croatia, on July 11, 1987, and was designated by the UN as the 5 billionth person living on Earth. In 1950 the world's population was only 2.5 billion – that means it has doubled in less than 50 years. Thanks to the UN's Food and Agriculture Organization (FAO), more and better food can be grown to feed all those people.

But doubling the world population so quickly means that food supply is still a huge problem. Farmers are often ignored when developing countries put their hopes in huge projects and cheap food for their cities. In 1974 the UN created the World Food Council (WFC), to give UN members advice on growing food, and the International Fund for Agricultural Development (IFAD), to pay for better seeds and tools. The World Food Programme (WFP) provides food to aid developing regions and helps countries where disasters have led to mass starvation, as was the case in Africa in the 1980s. In 1987 the United Nations Fund for Population Activities (UNFPA) finally decided to support family planning and birth control as a way of reducing Earth's population.

Complaints, complaints

In 1960 the UN announced that the next ten years would be the Decade for Development. All members would put a great emphasis on development so that a lot would be achieved. When the 1960s ended, the UN announced a second Decade for Development. The 1990s are the fourth. Obviously not enough has been accomplished in any of these decades. Have members found it too difficult to change?

Poorer countries don't think that the rich countries are listening. They know they would not be so poor if they were treated more fairly. When they borrow money from richer countries, they have to pay it back at high interest rates. When they export products, they can't sell them for a fair price. As well, most aid given to foreign countries has to benefit the giver, too. For instance, when Canada gives tools or equipment to other countries, it insists that they be manufactured in Canada so more Canadians will have jobs making them.

Some of the roadblocks to development are put up by the developing countries themselves. Richer countries complain that their help is often wasted because Third World governments want huge, expensive projects that hurt the environment. Local customs can create problems for UN workers, and corrupt local officials sometimes steal the money or goods provided.

Sometimes it is hard for rich and poor countries to work together. Developed countries don't like being scolded by newer UN members. After all, they pay most of the money for the UN and its development programs. Developing nations

The UN helps people in countries such as East Senegal, Africa, by providing mining equipment and know-how.

The World Bank is financing the building of the Tarbala Dam in Pakistan to help the people of the area.

attacked South Africa for mistreating its people but they were outraged when reports showed they sometimes treat their own citizens cruelly.

The United States especially resents criticism from new UN members – after all, it paid more than a quarter of the UN's costs. In the 1980s the American government refused to pay more than a fifth of the UN's budget unless the organization became more efficient and responsible. Other countries also failed to pay. There was talk of moving the organization away from New York.

Canada did all that it could to help the UN with its financial crisis, but most Canadians knew that some of these criticisms were fair. The UN had too many organizations – many more than have been listed here. Big international conferences cost a lot and did little. As well, rich countries had their own problems, and citizens who wanted them tackled first.

LISA BELZAK

"Only through education can we continue to improve the quality of life permanently in developing countries," says Lisa Belzak. She feels that working for the UN is the best way she can help educate people. So Belzak worked on the United Nations Transitional Authority in Cambodia (UNTAC) in 1992–93 supervising elections to make sure they were fair, and was a UN observer in the first multi-racial elections in South Africa in 1994. "Many times we had to negotiate with under-fed, under paid and heavily armed soldiers for the right to pass check-points on rural roads," says Belzak. "No guns were ever fired at me, but a friend working in a nearby village was killed."

Despite the dangers, Belzak continues to work for the UN because she believes that "with support from its member countries, the UN may be able to find a peaceful solution to political problems in developing countries."

UN organizations that help developing countries

Here are just a few of the UN's development organizations that help around the world.

THE FOOD AND AGRICULTURE ORGANIZATION (FAO)

Growing more food and sharing it more equally are two good ways to keep more people from starving. The UN created the FAO to help countries do both these things. Its headquarters is in Rome and its experts are busy everywhere in the world. The FAO has helped bring about a huge increase in world food production.

THE WORLD HEALTH ORGANIZATION (WHO)

Long before the UN was created, countries realized that sickness does not stop at national boundaries. Health is a world problem. The WHO headquarters at Geneva helps countries fight such worldwide plagues as malaria, smallpox and polio, and now struggles with AIDS (Acquired Immune Deficiency Syndrome).

THE UNITED NATIONS HIGH COMMISSION FOR REFUGEES (UNHCR)

Caring for refugees was a major concern during and after World War II. From 1943 to 1946 the UN Relief and Rehabilitation Administration (UNRRA) housed and fed 6 million refugees. In 1946 the International Refugee Organization (IRO) took over the job. In 1951 the UN appointed a High Commissioner for Refugees to try to solve the problem in three years. But in 1995 the High Commissioner, Sadako Ogata, is still busy as ever! Her office has won two Nobel Prizes for its work, in 1954 and 1981.

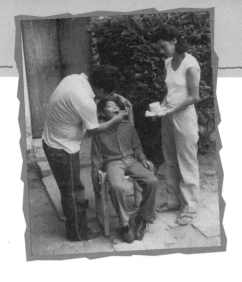

THE INTERNATIONAL BANK FOR RECONSTRUCTION AND DEVELOPMENT (IBRD)

This bank is also known as the World Bank. It's based in Washington and it helps members find money to build and rebuild factories, railways and ports. Linked to the World Bank is the International Monetary Fund (IMF). The IMF makes sure that its members' money is accepted by other countries. That means it can stop countries from borrowing if they can't pay back what they owe.

THE UNITED NATIONS CHILDREN'S FUND (UNICEF)

In 1976, UNICEF started a plan in 119 developing countries to help children. Kids were provided with medicine, food, clean water and an education. UNICEF still moves fast when children are in danger. In 1989, its Operation Lifeline was able to send 100 000 t (tons) of food and relief to the southern Sudan in just three months. UNICEF depends on the generosity of governments and on ordinary people who buy its greeting cards and other gift items.

THE UNITED NATIONS DEVELOPMENT PROGRAM (UNDP)

Begun in 1966, the UNDP coordinates the work of more than 13 UN agencies, from the FAO to the International Research and Training Institute for the Advancement of Women (INSTRAW) in San Domingo. Its main goal is to spread information, education and training. The UNDP sponsors the UN Volunteers, a program that sends skilled volunteers to work for two years in other countries. It also has several special funds, such as the UN Development Fund for Women (UNIFEM).

THE UN DISASTER RELIEF ORGANIZATION (UNDRO)

Almost any country can be hit by disaster, from radiation leaks, as in the Chernobyl nuclear power station in Ukraine in 1988, to earthquakes and hurricanes. Since 1972, UNDRO has organized help when a member has been hit hard. This organization also helps in continuing crises, such as the drought that hit 22 nations in the Sudan-Sahel region of Africa. Ethiopia, Somalia, Ghana and Nigeria have also been helped by the United Nations Sudano-Sahelian Office (UNSO).

Chapter 5

YOUR RIGHTS

What can you do when something happens that doesn't seem fair? Sometimes you can complain to a parent or a teacher or even a friend. Maybe you could get justice from your neighbourhood association. If you are a Canadian, you can also turn to the UN.

Sandra Lovelace didn't think it was fair that a Native man could bring his non-Native wife to live on a reserve when, according to Canada's Indian Act, a Native woman couldn't bring in her non-Native husband. The United Nations Human Rights Committee didn't think it was fair either. Canada had to change the law.

Gordon McIntyre didn't think it was right that a Quebec law stopped him from putting up a sign over his business in English, or even in English and French. The UN's Human Rights Committee agreed with him, too.

Canada is one of a few UN members that let their citizens take their grievances to the UN. Our Charter of Rights and Freedoms guarantees that all Canadians will enjoy equality and all the rights that are "reasonable" in a free and democratic society. But even Canada can do better.

The Universal Declaration

Canada and all the other UN members adopted a Universal Declaration of Human Rights on December 10, 1948. That date became known as Human Rights Day. The Declaration was called universal because that means it applies to everyone on Earth, whatever their race, sex, religion, etc.

The Declaration was as important as the UN's Charter. If the world was to be spared another terrible war, the horrors that brought the war must be ended, too. Six million Jews and millions of others whom Hitler considered unfit had died in his concentration camps. The horror of Hitler's regime had forced countries to fight. If the UN was to be taken seriously, it must defend human rights.

A Canadian, John Humphrey, helped write the Declaration. When a Russian delegate complained that the Declaration seemed to make people free of government, Humphrey agreed. "The struggle for human rights," he said, "has always been and always will be a struggle against authority."

Unfortunately, governments can't be forced to follow the Declaration. But even if it's not the law, it is a goal all countries can aim for.

What the Declaration says

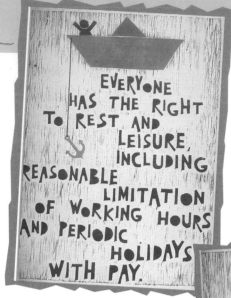

EVERYONE HAS THE RIGHT TO REST AND LEISURE, INCLUDING REASONABLE LIMITATION OF WORKING HOURS AND PERIODIC HOLIDAYS WITH PAY.

- You are entitled to life, freedom and to feel safe.
- You must be free from slavery, torture and cruel punishment.
- You are equal to anyone else as far as our laws are concerned.
- You cannot be arrested without good reason and you are entitled to a fair trial.
- You have a right to move, to marry, to start a family and to own property.
- You are free to think what you want and to follow your own religion.
- You have the right to say your opinion, to meet in groups and to take part in government.

EVERYONE HAS THE RIGHT TO LIFE, LIBERTY AND SECURITY OF PERSON.

Just as important, you have what are called social rights. That means you have the right to earn a living and to get help if you can't. You have a right to have fun and take part in community activities. You have the right to an education and food and shelter. But if you want these rights, you also have responsibilities to the community, such as obeying laws and voting.

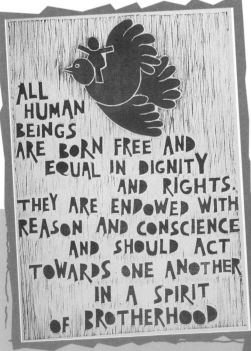

ALL HUMAN BEINGS ARE BORN FREE AND EQUAL IN DIGNITY AND RIGHTS. THEY ARE ENDOWED WITH REASON AND CONSCIENCE AND SHOULD ACT TOWARDS ONE ANOTHER IN A SPIRIT OF BROTHERHOOD

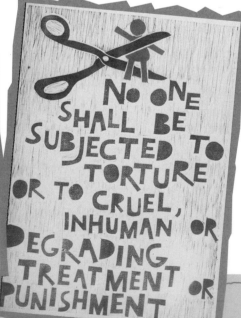

NO ONE SHALL BE SUBJECTED TO TORTURE OR TO CRUEL, INHUMAN OR DEGRADING TREATMENT OR PUNISHMENT

Putting the Declaration in action

Everyone knew when the Declaration was written in 1948 that it was one thing to declare human rights and quite another to make them a fact of daily life. For example, even though all the UN's members said that men and women had equal rights, only 32 of the original members allowed women to vote in elections. The job of making the Declaration work was given to the UN's Economic and Social Council (ECOSOC).

In 1946 ECOSOC created a Commission on Human Rights. Today its 43 member countries meet every year at Geneva to hear reports, make agreements on human rights problems and condemn cruel acts, such as torture. A Commission on the Status of Women, also created in 1946, looks at the same issues as they affect women.

The Universal Declaration of Human Rights recognized both individual rights and group rights. On December 16, 1966, the UN adopted two agreements called International Covenants, one concerning economic, social and cultural rights and the other on civil and political rights. Canada agreed to let its citizens bring complaints to the Human Rights Committee that watches over the Covenant on Civil and Political Rights.

For many years blacks in South Africa had almost no human rights.

Expanding human rights

The Universal Declaration didn't mention colonies, but in 1952 the General Assembly agreed "self-determination" was important for human rights. (Self-determination means the right of a country or group to decide how to be governed.) As former colonies gained influence in the UN, they persuaded the General Assembly to back an International Convention on the Elimination of all Forms of Racial Discrimination. Their main target was South Africa, with its cruel policy of apartheid. And it worked – by 1993, pressure by UN members persuaded South Africa's white minority to share power with the black majority.

The UN couldn't do much to fight human rights abuses in such powerful member countries as China or the Soviet Union, but it could stand up for some groups. For instance, the UN declared 1975 International Women's Year and the General Assembly declared 1976–1985 the International Decade for Women. The goals of this decade were to increase women's rights, recognize women's importance and bring an end to their brutal treatment by men.

The success of Women's Year encouraged supporters of human rights to spotlight other groups. In 1975 the General Assembly declared that disabled persons, not mentioned in the Universal Declaration, have the same rights as other people. The International Year of Disabled Persons, 1981, led to a Decade of Disabled Persons from 1983 to 1992. The United Nations Youth Fund grew out of the International Youth Year in 1985. After almost 30 years of hard work, largely by Polish and Canadian delegates, a Covenant on Children's Rights was adopted in 1991 at a conference chaired by Prime Minister Brian Mulroney of Canada.

Because they feared violence in their own country, about 250 000 Rwandan refugees poured into Tanzania in 1994.

Young girls doing school work in Nepal

Human rights aren't easy to agree on

You may think that human rights are obvious. Who could argue against holding elections or being able to say what you think or having enough to eat? But often rights conflict with other beliefs. For instance, most people believe that women should have the same rights as men. Yet many people share a religion that says that only men can be priests. Most people think jobs should be given to people without considering their race or sex. But isn't it also fair to help people get jobs when they and people like them have been barred in the past? Or does that discriminate against the people who already have the jobs?

You have the right to free speech, but should anyone have the right to say that some people are inferior because of their race or colour? These are some of the difficult problems the UN and its committees have to struggle with.

ADELAIDE SINCLAIR

The Canadian who has been involved longest in a top position with the United Nations Children's Fund (UNICEF) is Adelaide Sinclair. From 1946 to 1956 she was Canada's representative to the UNICEF Executive Board and she chaired the board from 1951 to 1952. In 1957 she became Deputy Executive-Director for UNICEF programs until she retired in 1967.

Sinclair originally got involved with UNICEF to find out more about the United Nations. UNICEF had been started as a temporary organization to help children in emergency situations created by World War II. But thanks to Sinclair and the UNICEF staff, the importance of UNICEF to help with the long-term needs of children in developing countries was realized, and the organization is still going strong.

49

Is the Declaration universal?

Since the 1960s, when dozens of nations and cultures became part of the UN, many have argued that the UN Universal Declaration is not really universal or worldwide. Other societies believe that it is more important for people to fit into the group they belong to than to do what suits them personally. For example, Canada's First Nations have a long tradition of respecting group needs. When Sandra Lovelace took her case to the UN (page 44), First Nations leaders argued that, once again, outsiders were telling them what is best.

In many countries, order is more important than the rules in the Universal Declaration. In Argentina, Brazil and other countries where there is a lot of terrorism, people have disappeared, never to be seen again. Later, mass graves revealed that most of the "disappeared" had been killed by police or soldiers. Shouldn't the UN get involved in this internal struggle? In 1990 the UN organized a huge military force to drive Iraqi invaders from Kuwait. But because it can't get involved in struggles inside a country, it cannot force Kuwait or other traditional Arab states to allow women to vote.

Canadians work for human rights throughout the world. In Toronto there is a centre where the victims of torture can go for medical treatment. A Canadian helped draft the Universal Declaration and another, Yvon Beaulne (see page 51), has headed the UN Human Rights Commission. Canadians helped African countries lead the struggle against apartheid in South Africa and against cruelty and injustice elsewhere.

Refugees and displaced persons in the former Yugoslavia

In 1992 the UN set up more than a dozen camps in Bangladesh for refugees from Myanmar (formerly Burma), but many still didn't have proper shelter.

Without the UN and the ideals of the Universal Declaration, would as much have happened to make the world a better place? And without the UN, could Sandra Lovelace and Gordon McIntyre have reminded us that Canada's record is not perfect?

YVON BEAULNE

Human rights were an interest of Yvon Beaulne even when he was a child. When he was growing up in Ontario, there was a law that prevented him from studying in French. That rule was later dropped, but it made him wonder how many other injustices there were in the world — and in Canada.

For nine years Beaulne served on the United Nations Human Rights Commission and made it a place where ordinary people could complain of injustice. He persuaded UN members to support the principle of freedom of religion even though some of them banned such freedoms at home. Beaulne publicly embarrassed countries where police and soldiers made people "disappear," never to be seen again. Finally, he turned a vague UN statement on the rights of children into a serious agreement. Yvon Beaulne made the UN listen to the victims of injustice.

Seeking safety from fighting in their country, refugees from Somalia arrive in Kenya.

Chapter 6

DOES THE UN HAVE A FUTURE?

Now you know why the UN was created in 1945. You've seen how it is organized and how it tackles three of the world's biggest problems: peace, development and human rights. Now comes the toughest question — has the UN been worthwhile?

Today's problems

On the one hand, the UN has sometimes ended fighting. But its peacekeeping missions are ignored whenever continuing hatreds turn to war. For instance, there are wars in the southern Sudan and in the Moslem republics of the former Soviet Union that are as terrible as anything in Somalia or Bosnia. However, TV crews haven't made countries or the UN concerned enough to intervene – even if anyone knew how to help.

The world's population is growing incredibly quickly. There will soon be three times as many people on Earth as there were in 1945, when the UN was founded. Most of them still go to bed hungry. Feeding these people and dealing with their pollution creates more problems. In the time it takes you to read this chapter, 40 hectares (100 acres) of rainforest in Brazil or Zaire will be cut down. Poor countries and many rich ones continue to pour poisons into the rivers and oceans that we all use.

Despite all the UN resolutions against slavery and torture, police in some countries still drag prisoners out of their cells to torture them into confessing their crimes. In some countries, women are whipped because of what they wear. In most countries, including Canada, women are not paid as much as men, no matter what the Universal Declaration says.

As for the UN itself, the need to include employees from every member nation means that UN offices are overstaffed and inefficient. A handful of dedicated people end up having to do the work of many others who see a UN job as a well-paid reward. In 1982, when the American government cut its financial support of the UN, the reason it gave was waste and corruption in the organization. Unfortunately for the UN, the former Soviet Union also cut its contributions because it couldn't afford them.

New expectations

When the Cold War ended in 1989, many people expected that the UN would be more active. Now that this dangerous situation was in the past, the UN wouldn't be stopped by deadlocks in discussions and could concentrate on solving other problems. Yet when the UN fought Iraqi attackers in Kuwait and killers in Somalia, many UN admirers were horrified. Baghdad, a great city in Iraq, was bombed in 1991. Somali people were shot in 1993 when they attacked UN soldiers. When Bosnia-Herzogovina found itself in a murderous civil war, many expected the UN to fight for one side against the others. But the UN was powerless because members refused to share in such a bloody war.

If wars and inefficiency are all there is to show for 50 years of the UN, why not start again or just forget it? Fifty years of UN committees and conferences and working groups, and all their resolutions have left the world in an utter mess. Or have they?

Who made the mess?

The UN never promised to meet all its goals. It promised only to try. It was never intended to govern the world. It is an association, with no more power than its members give it. If UN members choose war, not discussion, or if they make life awful for their own people, the UN can't stop them. It can only make sure that the rest of the world knows what is going on.

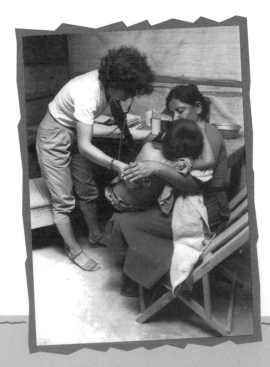

A child from El Salvador gets help from a doctor in a refugee camp in Honduras.

Children in many developing countries have to work hard to earn money for food. These children working at a brick factory may earn only 6¢ for a whole day's work.

And the UN has done much more than this. Because the UN was a place where East and West could talk, the Cold War never became hot. South Africa's apartheid system was squeezed out of existence. The UN organized experts who have doubled world food production, controlled the killer tropical disease malaria, and spread knowledge wherever it was wanted. If there is always more to do, maybe that's because an ever-growing population desperately needs more.

Throughout its 50 years, the UN has kept changing to meet new needs. It saw the need for a system of law for outer space. And for "inner space" too — UN members have already created a law of the sea to govern mining the seabeds for resources!

This emergency camp was set up by the UN to house 2 million Palestinian refugees.

UNITED NATIONS WORLD HERITAGE SITES

World Heritage Sites are areas chosen by the United Nations Educational, Scientific and Cultural Organization (UNESCO) as having special national, cultural or environmental importance. Canada has ten sites:
• L'Anse aux Meadows National Historic Park, Newfoundland
• Anthony Island Provincial Park, British Columbia
• Burgess Shale Site, British Columbia
• Dinosaur Provincial Park, Alberta
• Gros Morne National Park, Newfoundland
• Head-Smashed-In-Buffalo-Jump, Alberta
• Kluane National Park, Yukon Territory
• Nahanni National Park, Northwest Territories
• Quebec City, Quebec (shown above)
• Wood Buffalo National Park, on the border of Alberta and the Northwest Territories

Making the UN better

When world leaders set up the UN in 1945, they learned from the problems of the old League of Nations. The UN needs to continue to learn, change and work better than it does today. Here are some things it needs to fix:

• The UN gives too much power to tiny members. At one time the UN had a rule that members had to be big enough to share the UN's peacemaking burden. That rule was dropped long ago. The way the General Assembly is now organized, countries such as Rwanda, Fiji or Denmark, with less than 5 per cent of the world's people, can outvote the rest of the Assembly. On the other hand, the 12 countries with 90 per cent of the world's population (including China, India and the United States) have only 12 votes out of 185.

• The end of the Cold War in 1989 gave the Security Council back the power it lost after World War II because of disagreements between its most important members, the United States and the Soviet Union. Yet it does not use its power well. Even though it runs more than a dozen peacekeeping and peacemaking operations, it hasn't managed to hire many experts or get much money. UN members who aren't part of the Security Council don't like its secret meetings. And some of the ten countries who are members are too small to share the burden of peacekeeping.

A soldier in the UN Protection Force playing with a child during the Yugoslav crisis, 1992

♦ The UN gives a special place to the great powers of 1945. But are they still great? The United States, Russia and China qualify because of their wealth, size and population, but what about Britain and France? In the 1990s, Germany and Japan together pay 21 per cent of the UN budget. Shouldn't they be permanent members of the Security Council? The Third World majority in the UN think India, Egypt, Nigeria and Brazil should be recognized too. Other countries would nominate Indonesia, since it has the fourth-largest population in the world (after China, India and the United States).

♦ Some people think that the Economic and Social Council (ECOSOC) is not needed. After all, its work is also done by the committees of the General Assembly. But delegates to ECOSOC enjoy the privileges of being ambassadors and few are willing to give that up. As well, ending ECOSOC would require unanimity

from the five great powers and a two-thirds majority in the Assembly, and getting so many countries to agree is unlikely.

♦ The UN has too many staff with high salaries and grand titles. Xavier Pérez de Cuéllar, the sixth Secretary-General, tried to solve this problem by cutting many important-sounding positions. Instead of 30 people reporting to the Secretary-General, only 8 do now. The problem is that member countries keep asking for more of the top-level jobs at the UN. When the people who are hired cannot do their work very well, they often need assistants to cover their mistakes. So more people end up being hired. The UN could also be more efficient if it combined many of its programs and agencies.

In 1984, Xavier Pérez de Cuéllar, Secretary-General (third from left), met with Canada's Prime Minister Pierre Trudeau (third from right) to discuss disarmament.

Canada needs the UN

There was a time when Canada seemed far away from much of the world. It used to take weeks by ship to come here from Asia or Europe. Now it takes a split second by telephone and just a few hours by plane. Canadians come from every part of the world. When people are killed in war or die of starvation anywhere in the world, some Canadians feel the pain. What happens to a rainforest in the tropics or a volcano in the Philippines affects Canada's climate. If a war spreads or if terrorists bring their violence here, Canadians are touched. That's why Canadian politicians and diplomats worked so hard at San Francisco in 1945 to start the UN, and they have been working hard for it ever since.

People do more damage to each other and to the environment than hundreds of UNs could cure. What the UN can do, with all its committees and agencies and meetings, is help people understand their problems and find better answers. After all, you have to see a problem before you can fix it. When the UN makes the world face a problem, it makes people worry, then work to find answers. And the problems that are probably doing the most damage may be the ones that haven't been noticed yet.

Back in your neighbourhood, life goes on. Sometimes your association is kept very busy stopping fights and helping families, and sometimes everyone gets along pretty well. You all agree that setting up the neighbourhood association was a good idea and that life is better, but still there always seem to be problems to deal with.

Air pollution can spread far beyond this factory in Romania to affect people in many other countries.

This Canadian medic is working for the United Nations Transitional Authority in Cambodia (UNTAC). He travels by boat to bring help to villages along the rivers.

The United Nations High Commission for Refugees (UNHCR) provides food and aid to many children, including these Angolan refugees in Zaire.

The world certainly has no shortage of problems either. But, like your neighbourhood, it always has problem solvers. Maybe you will be one of the people who finds the right answers to the world's biggest problems. Thanks to the UN, you have a way of getting started. Of course, keeping the world together will be difficult. It will take patience, persuasion and a lot of give and take. But nothing worthwhile is ever easy.

This mother is trying to keep her children fed and safe in a UN camp for displaced persons in Azerbaijan.

Canada's prime minister, William Lyon Mackenzie King, speaking at the San Francisco Conference in 1945

Preamble to the Charter of the United Nations

WE THE PEOPLES OF THE UNITED NATIONS

determined

> to save succeeding generations from the scourge of war, which twice in our lifetime has brought untold sorrow to mankind, and

> to reaffirm faith in fundamental human rights, in the dignity and worth of the human person, in the equal rights of men and women and of nations large and small, and

> to establish conditions under which justice and respect for the obligations arising from treaties and other sources of international law can be maintained, and

> to promote social progress and better standards of life in larger freedom,

and for these ends

> to practice tolerance and live together in peace with one another as good neighbours, and

> to unite our strength to maintain international peace and security, and

> to ensure, by the acceptance of principles and the institution of methods, that armed force shall not be used, save in the common interest, and

> to employ international machinery for the promotion of the economic and social advancement of all peoples,

have resolved to combine our efforts to accomplish these aims.

accordingly, our respective Governments, through representatives assembled in the city of San Francisco, who have exhibited their full powers found to be in good and due form, have agreed to the present Charter of the United Nations and do hereby establish an international organization to be known as the United Nations.

The United Nation's Secretaries-General

(and their terms of office)

Boutros Boutros-Ghali of Egypt
1992–

Xavier Pérez de Cuéllar of Peru
1982–1991

Kurt Waldheim of Austria
1972–1981

U Thant of Burma
(now Myanmar) 1961–1971

Dag Hammerskjöld of Sweden
1953–1961

Trygve Lie of Norway
1946–1953

Glossary

allies: organizations or countries that join together. The Allied countries were the countries fighting Germany and its allies in World Wars I and II.

ambassador: a top official representing her country in other countries

apartheid: the South African policy that discriminated against blacks

bloc: countries or groups that share the same purpose or beliefs

boycott: refusal to deal with a business or country in order to protest something that business or country has done

civil war: a war in which people of the same country fight each other

Cold War: rivalry between countries that stops just short of actual war

colony: a country that is ruled by another country

communism: a system of government based on the idea that people should work according to their ability and receive money or aid according to their needs

delegate: a person chosen to speak and act for a group or country

diplomat: a person who represents his government in its business with other governments

disarmament: a reduction of a country's military forces or weapons

East: the Communist countries of eastern Europe

nation: a group of people organized under one government; a country

refugee: a person fleeing from her country, or driven out by the dangers of war or cruel treatment

republic: a country governed by representatives elected by the country's people. Canada is a republic.

revolution: a sudden overthrow of a government or political system

Third World: the developing nations of Africa, Asia and South America

veto: the right of a government to reject a bill and prevent its enactment

West: the non-Communist countries of Europe and North America

Index

977